LAKE CLASSICS

Great American Short Stories III

Edna
FERBER

Stories retold by C.D. Buchanan
Illustrated by James Balkovek

LAKE EDUCATION
Belmont, California

LAKE CLASSICS

Great American Short Stories I

Washington Irving, Nathaniel Hawthorne, Mark Twain, Bret Harte, Edgar Allan Poe, Kate Chopin, Willa Cather, Sarah Orne Jewett, Sherwood Anderson, Charles W. Chesnutt

Great American Short Stories II

Herman Melville, Stephen Crane, Ambrose Bierce, Jack London, Edith Wharton, Charlotte Perkins Gilman, Frank R. Stockton, Hamlin Garland, O. Henry, Richard Harding Davis

Great American Short Stories III

Thomas Bailey Aldrich, Irvin S. Cobb, Rebecca Harding Davis, Theodore Dreiser, Alice Dunbar-Nelson, Edna Ferber, Mary Wilkins Freeman, Henry James, Ring Lardner, Wilbur Daniel Steele

Great British and Irish Short Stories

Arthur Conan Doyle, Saki (H. H. Munro), Rudyard Kipling, Katherine Mansfield, Thomas Hardy, E. M. Forster, Robert Louis Stevenson, H. G. Wells, John Galsworthy, James Joyce

Great Short Stories from Around the World

Guy de Maupassant, Anton Chekhov, Leo Tolstoy, Selma Lagerlöf, Alphonse Daudet, Mori Ogwai, Leopoldo Alas, Rabindranath Tagore, Fyodor Dostoevsky, Honoré de Balzac

Cover and Text Designer: Diann Abbott

Library of Congress Catalog Number: 95-76750
ISBN 1-56103-068-6
Printed in the United States of America
1 9 8 7 6 5 4 3 2 1

CONTENTS

❦ Lake Classic Short Stories ❦

"The universe is made of stories, not atoms."
　　　　　—Muriel Rukeyser

"The story's about you."
　　　　　—Horace

Everyone loves a good story. It is hard to think of a friendlier introduction to classic literature. For one thing, short stories are *short*—quick to get into and easy to finish. Of all the literary forms, the short story is the least intimidating and the most approachable.

Great literature is an important part of our human heritage. In the belief that this heritage belongs to everyone, *Lake Classic Short Stories* are adapted for today's readers. Lengthy sentences and paragraphs are shortened. Archaic words are replaced. Modern punctuation and spellings are used. Many of the longer stories are abridged. In all the stories, painstaking care has been taken to preserve the author's unique voice.

Lake Classic Short Stories have something for everyone. The hundreds of stories in the collection cover a broad terrain of themes, story types, and styles. Literary merit was a deciding factor in story selection. But no story was included unless it was as enjoyable as it was instructive. And special priority was given to stories that shine light on the human condition.

Each book in the *Lake Classic Short Stories* is devoted to the work of a single author. Little-known stories of merit are included with famous old favorites. Taken as a whole, the collected authors and stories make up a rich and diverse sampler of the story-teller's art.

Lake Classic Short Stories guarantee a great reading experience. Readers who look for common interests, concerns, and experiences are sure to find them. Readers who bring their own gifts of perception and appreciation to the stories will be doubly rewarded.

❧ Edna Ferber ❧
(1887–1968)

About the Author

As a girl in Appleton, Wisconsin, Edna Ferber wanted to be an actress rather than a writer. But when her father became blind, 17-year-old Edna had to get a job. She quickly found work as a reporter on Appleton's newspaper, the *Daily Crescent*.

Seeing her talent, her editor at the newspaper encouraged her to keep writing. But Edna was not happy with her first story. She threw the whole book away. Her mother pulled it from the garbage and sent it to a publisher. In 1921, it came out as Ferber's first novel, *Dawn O'Hara*.

In 1924, the novel *So Big* made Ferber a best-selling author. It also earned her a Pulitzer Prize. There were more bestsellers to follow. Her novels *Show Boat*, *Cimarron*, and *Giant* became hit motion pictures, along with many another of her books. *Show Boat* also had a long run as a musical on Broadway. Ferber wrote stage plays, too, teaming up with playwright George S. Kaufman.

Ferber's tales take place in many settings. *Cimarron* tells about the 1889 land rush in Oklahoma. *American Beauty* describes the lives of Polish immigrants in Connecticut. *Come and Get It* is about the logging business in Wisconsin. *Giant* takes readers to Texas and *Ice Palace* to Alaska.

Perhaps Ferber's early interest in the theater led her to write stories that were ideal for the stage and screen. Her work was once described as "written ready-made for the movies, lacking nothing but the Technicolor."

As you read, try to imagine these stories on the big screen.

Representing
T. A. Buck

A traveling saleswoman's
life has never been easy.
Especially 80 years ago. In
this charming story you will
meet the unforgettable
Emma McChesney. Read on
for some insights into the
mind and heart of a hard-
charging career woman.

THE BEAUTY OF THE MUSIC BROUGHT HOT TEARS TO
EMMA'S EYES.

Representing T. A. Buck

Emma McChesney swung off the 2:15 train and ran for the hotel bus. To get inside, the trim, good-looking young woman had to climb over four feet. Two belonged to a fat man in brown. The other two belonged to a lean man in black. She knew why they were hogging the end seats. If they got off first at the hotel, they would get first choice of the best rooms available.

The bus smelled of mold and tobacco. Emma McChesney had spent nine years on the road. She was what people called a "drummer." As a traveling salesperson, it was her job to drum up business. She was used to the smell of buses.

Emma glanced at the fat traveling man. He was a picture in brown. He wore a brown suit, brown shoes, brown scarf, and a brown hat. Peeping over the edge of his pocket was a handkerchief with a brown border. He looked like a giant chocolate fudge.

"I'll bet he sells coffins and other undertakers' supplies," thought Emma. "And the other one—the tall, lanky one in black—I suppose his line would be sheet music. Or maybe it's phonographs. Or perhaps he's going to give a talk for the Young Men's Sunday Evening Club."

Emma's product line was ladies' underwear. She worked for T.A. Buck's Featherloom Skirt Company. During her years on the road, she had picked up a thing or two on human nature. She was not surprised to see the fat man and the thin man leap out of the bus. They were into the hotel before she had time to straighten her hat. By the time she reached the desk, the two had registered.